ATALANTA

ATALANTA

THE FASTEST RUNNER IN THE WORLD

Written by Priscilla Galloway
Illustrated by Normand Cousineau

Annick Press Ltd.
Toronto • New York

© 1995 Priscilla Galloway (text)
© 1995 Normand Cousineau (art)
Designed by Primeau Dupras

Annick Press Ltd.

Annick Press gratefully acknowledges the support of the Canada Council
and the Ontario Arts Council.

Canadian Cataloguing in Publication Data
Galloway, Priscilla, 1930-
Atalanta, the fastest runner in the world

(Tales of ancient lands)
ISBN 1-55037-401-X

1. Atalanta (Greek mythology) - Juvenile literature.
I. Cousineau, Normand. II. Title. III. Series:
Galloway, Priscilla, 1930- . Tales of ancient lands.

PS8563.A45A92 1995   j398.21   C95-930868-7   PZ8.1.G35At 1995

The art in this book was rendered in ink and gouache.
The text was typeset in Perpetua and Lithos.

Distributed in Canada by: Firefly Books Ltd.
250 Sparks Avenue, Willowdale, ON M2H 2S4

Published in the U.S.A. by Annick Press (U.S.) Ltd.
Distributed in the U.S.A. by:
Firefly Books (U.S.) Inc.
P.O. Box 1338, Ellicott Station, Buffalo, NY 14205

Printed and bound in Canada by Metropole Litho, Montréal

To Bart, who
was ten years
old the summer
I began Atalanta,
and loved the
story right from
its very first
draft, and to
Bronwyn, who
loves all my
Greek stories.

P.C.

To my mother,
her daughters
and her
granddaughters.

N.C.

CONTENTS

PROLOGUE

Atalanta had a very bad start in life. As a newborn baby, she was carried to a lonely hillside and left there. She could be eaten by a wild animal, or she could starve to death. If she was lucky, she could be found and raised, most likely as a slave.

Why did this happen? Atalanta's father decided not to keep the baby, and by Greek law and custom at the time he had that right. In ancient Greece, a baby had no rights until the father officially accepted him or her as a member of the family.

We think of the Greeks as civilized people. They had great respect for freedom, along with equally great respect for law and order, for community. How could such people put an infant out to die?

There is no easy answer and no single answer. We don't think like these ancient people. To some extent we can only guess why they did what they did.

Sometimes survival of the family must have been at stake. Families grew or hunted for their own food, wove woollen cloth from the fleece of their own sheep to make their clothing, tanned leather for their sandals, and built their own homes. Ordinary people were lucky if they had enough food, a few clothes, and a place to live. If the crops failed or the hunting was bad, everybody went hungry. However painfully, a parent might decide that a quick death for an infant would be better than slow starvation for the whole family. The ancient Greeks were a practical people.

There were other reasons as well. Sometimes there were too many children. A family couldn't provide for all of them. Sometimes a child was disabled or deformed. Physical perfection was very important to the Greeks. A disabled child was a disgrace. If a family already had a girl or two, another baby girl might not be wanted. Girls were expensive, especially when they got married. The father of the bride had to pay money to the father of the groom. Atalanta's father didn't want a daughter at all. He wanted sons.

Often a family must have found it a horrendous choice.

Most babies were loved and welcomed by their families right from the start. Once the baby was officially accepted, he or she could not be abandoned. Even if the birth family did not accept a baby, the gods might save the child's life. In stories, they always did. No doubt many parents hoped that real life would turn out the same way.

Gods and goddesses were everywhere in that ancient world. Belief was strong and unquestioning, uncontested by logic and scientific observation. To those people, the gods were real. Every tree and every stream had its spirit. Gods did not have to appear in their own form. They might take the form of a friend or relative, or they might appear in a dream. Gods loved, or argued, or fought with each other much as people might do, but in more powerful ways. Sometimes people would get caught in struggles between one god and another. A particular god could be a person's enemy or friend. Atalanta had a special connection with the goddess Artemis, the virgin huntress, but she broke it when she fell in love. She knew Artemis would be angry. Artemis was no friend of Aphrodite, the goddess of Love.

The Greeks told stories and made plays about their gods and goddesses, their heroes and heroines. They told stories to explain their world. Greek stories interpreted the people's feelings and experiences, so the stories became fused with the real world and part of it. A hunter might not be much surprised to hear a god's voice in the forest or feel a goddess holding his arm steady and guiding his arrow on its way.

This may have been partly because the stories were told, not read. People loved to listen to plays and stories told in poetry. It was natural for them to connect the stories to their own experiences and feelings, to make them real. Through the ages, ideas, images, characters, and stories from Greek literature have inspired authors — first in Europe and later in North America — as Atalanta, with all her conflicts of love and loyalty, inspired me.

MT. OLYMPUS

TROY

AEGEAN SEA

GREECE

DELPHI

CALYDON

ITHACA

ASIA MINOR

ATHENS

MYCENAE

LACONIA

SPARTA

MEDITERRANEAN SEA

TO CYCLOPS

CRETE

PRONUNCIATION OF
GREEK NAMES

Greek names are not as difficult as they look. Sound the letters the way you do in English, except as follows.

RULE	EXAMPLE	SOUND
c is usually pronounced as k	Socrates	Sok'-ra-teez
final e is not silent	Clymene	Kly'-muh-nee
g is usually hard, as in "gas"	Meleager	Mel-ee-ay'-ger
ae and oe are pronounced "ee"	Oeneus	Ee'-nee-us

Sometimes it's hard to know where to put the stress. "Atalanta," "Telamon" and "Saurus" sound just the way they would in English. Say the other names like this:

Merope	Meh'-roh-pee
Melanion	Meh-lay'-nee-un
Iasus	Eye-ay'-sus
Aphrodite	Af-ro-di'-tee

CHAPTER ONE

A BEAR
AND A BABY

his is a story about Atalanta. Atalanta lived a long time ago, in western Greece, in the region of Calydon. She was a hunter and a runner.

Her father, Iasus, had wanted a boy. He was so angry when his wife gave birth to a girl that he ordered his shepherd to leave her out on a hillside to die. "Go at least two days' journey from here," he commanded. "The autumn nights are cold, and the animals are hungry. The end will come quickly, no doubt."

The shepherd took the baby. "I'm sorry for her," he told his wife, "but it can't be helped."

Luckily, the goddess Artemis was out hunting that day and heard the baby crying. Artemis was not a kind goddess. She would not have bothered to save a baby boy, but she liked the tiny girl. She knew this child would be important to her.

The hills and the lands around them were rocky and desolate, no good for farming. Nobody lived there, except for one little family, Telamon and Merope, and Telamon's best friend Saurus. As usual, Saurus and Telamon were hunting that day. Artemis changed herself into a deer and let them see her.

The hunters set their dogs loose and ran in pursuit. For an hour they ran through scrub brush and stunted trees, scratched by blackberry bushes, sliding sometimes and tripping in patches of loose gravel. Again and again they glimpsed the deer. Once Telamon even raised his bow. Then suddenly the deer vanished. The dogs whimpered and cowered on the ground. The two men stood still and listened.

"What's that?" Saurus was puzzled. "It's not a deer, that's certain. And what's wrong with the dogs?" They could both hear a sort of snuffling noise, and a thin, wailing cry.

"Almost sounds like a baby, doesn't it," said Telamon. He followed Saurus toward the sound.

"Stop!" Saurus barely breathed the word, but Telamon instantly obeyed. Not twenty paces away, a huge brown bear faced them. The bear raised its head. Then it reared up on two feet and stood, looking down at them. Its sharp, curved claws were extended. Telamon's nostrils curled with its musty smell. Both men knew immediately why the dogs had given up the chase. The thin, wailing cry continued. Again Saurus grabbed Telamon's arm. He pointed. At the bear's feet lay a tiny bundle.

"Shsssh," whispered Saurus. The two men looked at each other. They looked

back at the bear and the little wailing creature at its feet. For a long minute, bear and men faced each other. All were still. Then the bear dropped down on all fours. Was that really a baby? Would the bear carry it away? Telamon wondered how fast he could get a shot at the beast. His arrow might only enrage it. The bear could easily kill him and Saurus and the baby as well. Slowly he raised his bow.

The bear looked at him. Very slowly, as if daring Telamon to shoot, the creature turned away. Then it moved quickly, clambering up the rocky hillside, and was gone. Telamon could feel the sweat dripping down his back. He and Saurus moved forward on unsteady legs.

Telamon knelt beside the baby, putting his hand carefully under the infant's neck and head. The little naked body was lying partly on a ragged piece of blanket. She had soiled the blanket, and Telamon cleaned her and it with moss as best he could before he picked her up and cuddled her in his arms.

At once her tiny hand grabbed his finger and held tight. Her face was red and blotchy from screaming and ant bites. Telamon smiled. "Ugly little thing," he said, "but she's not giving up, is she? I'll take her. If she lives, she can help out at home."

His wife Merope was furious. "A baby! You've done a lot of stupid things, Telamon, but this is the stupidest. I'm not looking after her. You can take her back where you found her."

"She wouldn't last the night," said Telamon. "Some animal – that bear, like as not – would have her for dinner."

"Let it," Merope replied.

Telamon held the baby. He tilted his wife's face so that she was looking at the child. The baby sucked desperately at Telamon's big, rough finger.

For the moment, her screams were stilled. All three people were silent.

"I'll take her if you command me. I'm a good wife, and I'll do my duty, even if I don't want to." Merope spoke calmly now. "I'd look after our baby if we had one, but we haven't. I wish we had a baby, Telamon, but this isn't the same. You brought her home. Keep her if you want. I won't get in your way. But please, don't ask me to help."

"That's all right," said Telamon. "I understand how you feel. There is plenty of goat's milk. Saurus and I will manage. Maybe you'll feel differently later."

"Hmph," sniffed Merope, and turned away.

It wasn't easy to hold the nanny goat so that the hungry baby could suck. Telamon needed Saurus to help. When Merope saw them, she roared with laughter. Her belly shook. For a while, she was laughing too hard to talk. "Men!" she gasped at last. "Don't you know anything? First you milk the goat. Then you dip a rag in the milk. Here, take this one. The baby sucks on the cloth. Dip and suck, just keep doing it." She shook her head, still chuckling. "Holding a nanny goat, Saurus! You do look silly." Then Merope's face grew tight. "But I'm not helping you," she said. She stamped her foot. "Get out of here, all of you."

Telamon and Saurus looked after the baby. They carried her with them while they hunted. Time passed. Telamon learned to draw his bow and line up his arrow while the little girl clung to his shoulders. "Stay still," he'd warn her, "don't move a muscle," and the child obeyed. They named her Atalanta, "unswaying," because she was so good at keeping still. As soon as she could toddle, Saurus made her arrows and a tiny bow. Both men would laugh and clap when she hit her target.

"You waste too much time on that child," Merope said sometimes. However, Telamon and Saurus were fond of her, and little Atalanta learned to help them. When they went after a wild boar, she carried the extra arrows and spears. She learned to track the animals they hunted, mostly deer, but sometimes small game like partridges or rabbits. She learned to move quietly in the forest. When she could hold a larger bow, she practised for long hours every day until she could hit her target oftener than Saurus. (She was never quite as good as Telamon.)

Merope beat Atalanta sometimes, though not often. "Your own parents threw you out to die," she told her. "Don't expect meat for dinner tonight. Porridge is good enough for you."

"Thank you, Merope," said Atalanta politely. "I like porridge." She knew that Telamon would save plenty of meat, more than she could eat, and give it to her quietly later. Many times she cried herself to sleep, all the same.

When Merope wanted her to clean house or cook, Atalanta tried to help. She swept the hard-packed dirt floor with all her strength. Little puffs of dust jumped in the golden sunlight. But accidents always happened. Once she tripped on the scrap bucket, sending vegetable peels and sour milk to make smelly trails in the pile of dust she had swept together on the floor. "There goes the pigs' dinner," Merope scolded. "Can't you do anything right?"

"I'm sorry, Merope." Atalanta rushed to pick up the bucket of water. Her hands slipped on the handle and water sloshed into the mess on the floor.

Merope grabbed the broom. Whack! Her blows landed on the child's back. "Out," she muttered between clenched teeth. "Get out of here. Useless brat. I don't know why Telamon puts up with you."

More time passed. Atalanta grew bigger. One day Merope's sister asked, "When is that girl going to stop hanging around with the men? When is she going to learn to spin yarn and weave cloth? She'll be ready to get married one of these days, but what man would want her for a wife?"

Merope listened. She talked to Atalanta. "Let's try something new," she said. "You're old enough to spin and weave. Weaving beautiful cloth is exciting work, just as exciting as hunting. Come and look at my design on the loom."

Telamon was pleased. At last his wife was accepting the girl he had brought home. He smiled at them. Perhaps now Atalanta would really be like a daughter to them both. "What a good idea," he said. "You are an expert weaver, Merope. Your cloth is even and fine. Nobody makes such complicated designs. Atalanta, you could not have a better teacher. It's time you learned to do things around the house."

Atalanta's heart sank. Body and soul, she had been formed by the forest and meadows, the sun and wind and rain. She hated being indoors. The house always felt like a prison, and she the clumsiest of prisoners. Merope often worked at her loom from morning to night. How could she bear it? But Telamon was right: Merope was a fine weaver.

"It is beautiful work," said Atalanta, "the way you do it. I'd like to be able to do that. I don't think I'd be any good, though," she added. "I'm sure my thread would break, or I'd get the colours wrong. I never do anything right in the house."

"Try your best," coaxed Telamon. "You won't be perfect to start with, but I'm sure you can learn."

Atalanta stayed indoors. Day after day, she loaded Merope's distaff and twirled Merope's spindle, but her yarn came out all thick and knobby. Day after day, she stood in front of Merope's loom and threw the shuttle through the long threads from one side to the other, but she couldn't see how the pattern was growing on the loom so that she could continue it, and her shuttle got stuck more often than not.

"My sister's girl can spin a fine, even thread. She weaves a good plain cloth, and she's two years younger than you," snapped Merope. "What's wrong with you, Atalanta? Don't you want to learn?"

Atalanta's head was bent so that Merope could not see her face. Her tears dripped quietly into her tangled yarn. "I can't spin," she sobbed. "I can't weave." Her fingers itched to hold her bow. Her legs ached to get out and run.

"What a mess!" Merope glowered. "Get out of the way, girl. I'll have to straighten it out for you again."

One night, when Atalanta was crying herself to sleep, the goddess Artemis appeared. She carried a silver bow. A golden quiver full of gleaming arrows was slung on her shoulder. "I've been keeping watch over you, Atalanta," the shining goddess told the child. "I knew from the time you were born that you would serve me well. Now you need my help. Listen." Atalanta lifted her tear-stained face.

"You will be a great hunter; this I promise you," continued Artemis. "You are lucky. Few mortals win my favour, few women and no men. You will always outrun the hounds. But one promise demands another. Atalanta, you must always follow my ways. I have never married. You

24

must not marry. Keep your body to yourself. You were not meant for love and for bearing children. You don't have to learn household tasks."

"Thank you, Goddess, thank you." Atalanta gulped and sniffled. "I hate sitting. I hate being indoors. I hate trying to do things I can't do. When I string my bow and let my arrow fly — that's when I feel alive. If I got married…" Atalanta stopped to think. The goddess looked at her and waited. "If I got married, I'd have to spin and weave, wouldn't I? No, I won't do that."

Artemis smiled and disappeared.

"That's a good story," laughed Merope the next day. "Goddesses don't bother with silly girls. Get to your loom, Atalanta. We'll try a very easy design. Anybody can do it."

"I believe you, Atalanta," said Telamon. "I've always wondered about that gigantic bear, back when Saurus and I found you. We thought it was going to kill you, but it could have done that easily before we came along. It could just as well have been keeping you safe from other animals."

"A giant bear!" Merope was startled. "Bears are sacred to Artemis, no animal more so. Why didn't you tell me about it?"

"I tried," grumbled Telamon. "It's not hard to know why Artemis the hunter would like you, Atalanta, when you're so good with your bow and arrows. Merope, we need to find out more about this, don't we. Saurus and I must go to Apollo's shrine at Delphi. We'll ask the oracle what Atalanta should do."

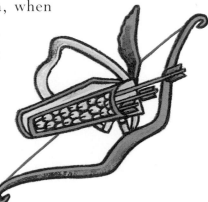

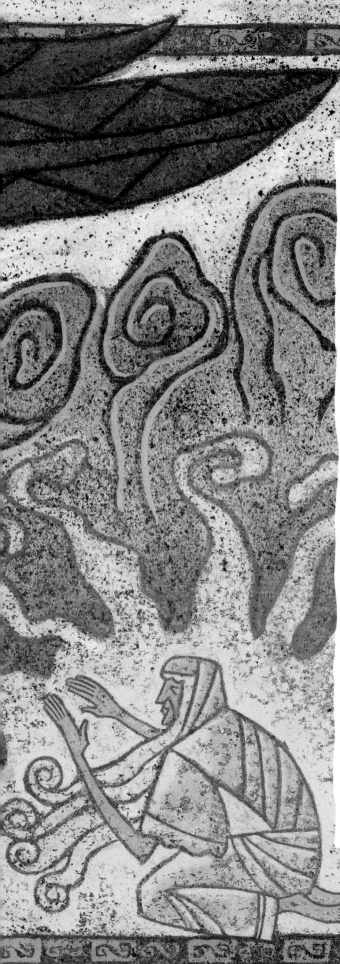

CHAPTER TWO

ADVICE FROM
THE ORACLE

Telamon had never travelled more than one day's journey away from home, Saurus had not been even as far away as Telamon. At first they walked through grassy meadows and groves of cypresses and oaks. Soon, however, their road grew rocky and steep. They moved fast enough on the first day, but slower and slower on the second.

"I need food," said Saurus.

"What I'd give for two or three fat quail," sighed Telamon. "We'll have to stop and hunt."

Just as he spoke, he looked toward the woods. A quick gesture warned Saurus to keep quiet. Carefully Telamon fitted an arrow against the string and drew back his bow. His arrow whizzed through the air and found its mark. A deer crumpled to the ground.

"I don't believe it!" exclaimed Saurus.

"We ask for food, and a deer comes to your arrow!"

"Surely Artemis is sending us food," said Telamon. "She wants us to make this trip."

"She's showing us her power," Saurus replied. "She frightens me."

When they reached Delphi, Saurus and Telamon sacrificed a lamb. A young priestess in white robes beckoned to them. They stumbled after her down a dark tunnel which widened suddenly into a vast, misty cavern. An ancient priestess crouched beside a small, bright fire.

Their guide piled a huge armful of green branches on the fire. Smoke eddied. Telamon and Saurus coughed and choked. Telamon wiped his eyes. "Brother of Artemis, great god Apollo," he asked, "tell us what Atalanta must do."

The priestess of the oracle swayed in the mist and smoke. Saurus sank to his knees. He leaned against his friend's legs. Telamon could feel him trembling. In the smoke, the priestess seemed solid one minute and ghostly the next. She seemed to grow taller and taller until she towered above them, then smaller and smaller again.

Time passed, how much or little neither man could ever say. Then a voice spoke through the mouth of the priestess. Long afterwards, Telamon or Saurus would try to tell what it was like. "We knew the voice was not human," they declared. "It wasn't the god Apollo, either. It was a soft and singing voice, and it went through our bodies quivering, like a silver javelin or a golden arrow. This is what we heard:

"'I am Artemis of the silver darts. I am fleet-footed Artemis. I ruled here long before my brother Apollo. Hear me and obey. I have set Atalanta free to follow the wind and woods, and to walk in the beds of streams and rivers. She does not serve Hestia, goddess of hearth and home, or Athene, goddess of weaving. Atalanta has promised her life to me.'"

Even Merope could not argue with the oracle. "Back to your hunting, then," she said. "But I warn you: Artemis is a cruel goddess. She demands much from those who serve her. Sometime you may hate your freedom. Sometime you may wish you had learned to weave."

Atalanta ran until every muscle ached. She threw herself down on the moss and buried her face in it. She loosened her tunic and let the sun warm her body. By a quiet pool she stripped and jumped in. Her strong hands rubbed and rubbed, washing away the smell and feel of the cramped and airless house.

Now she was up at dawn every day. With her bow and arrows, she roamed the countryside. However long it took, she never came home without some game. When Telamon broke his leg in a fall, Atalanta kept the stew pot full of meat.

Once she hunted all day without stopping to eat or drink. It was getting dark, and she was dizzy from thirst, but she couldn't find any water. At last she dashed her staff against a rock. "Great Artemis, send me water," she cried. At once, a spring of water gushed out. Atalanta cupped her hands and drank. Deep thankfulness flooded through her. This is how my life is going  to be, she thought, a quiet life of hunting and running. With the protection of Artemis, at last she felt secure.

Atalanta had no idea that the great adventures of her life were just about to begin.

CHAPTER THREE

THE GREAT BOAR HUNT

nly a few months later, Oeneus, King of Calydon, sent out a call for help. He had forgotten to sacrifice a lamb to Artemis that spring. "You honoured the other gods," said Artemis, "and you forgot to honour me. You'll be sorry." In her anger, the goddess sent a wild boar to trample the corn and the grape vines. It attacked sheep and cattle as well. The shepherds and herdsmen could not save them.

Many great heroes came from far away. Some of them carried long spears to thrust at the boar, while others had armed themselves with axes and knives. Others carried light javelins, ready to throw. Atalanta also came to the hunt, armed with her bow and arrows. Meleager, the king's son, was in charge, but he could not get all the hunters to work together. His two uncles were part

of the problem. "Make sure you put us in the place of honour," one of them commanded. "We expect to be right at the front."

"Why did the king put you in charge of the hunt, Meleager?" the other asked rudely. "We've been fighting wild boars since before you were born."

"Fighting with everybody else too," muttered the man beside Atalanta. "I hope they keep their spears for the boar today."

Atalanta was part of the problem too.

"I won't hunt with a woman," one man insisted.

"I won't either," chimed in another. "Hunting is men's business."

Meleager thought fast. Everybody was questioning his authority. If he gave in now, they would not respect him. He'd heard that Atalanta was a good hunter. Were the others jealous? He glanced toward the slim woman who stood modestly apart from the crowd, then looked back at the two men.

"Is her aim better than yours?" he asked them quietly. "Is her arm stronger? Go or stay, just as you like. You can't win the trophy if you don't take part in the game."

The two men grumbled, but they did not leave. The king had promised the boar's hide and tusks to whoever could kill the beast, and all the great hunters wanted the reward and the glory for themselves. They pushed and jostled each other to get to the front and centre of the group, Meleager's uncles most of all.

Atalanta stayed out of the way. She didn't care about glory, or a reward. The boar had gored people and destroyed crops. It had killed two children whom she knew. All she cared about was helping to kill it. Atalanta flexed her arms. She could feel the blood flowing, the energy surging in her body. Every muscle was ready for action. "Thank you for my body, great Artemis," she breathed. "Guide my arm well today, that's all I ask." She looked at the other hunters, still pushing and shoving each other. "There must be something about this kind of hunting that I don't know," she thought. "Why are all those men bunching together like that? When the boar rushes at them, they won't have room to hurl a javelin or shoot an arrow. They're going to hurt each other."

Meleager's eyes kept straying toward Atalanta. "She stands like a deer," he thought, "ready to run." The wild boar, the noisy hunters, and his own hard task faded right out of his mind as he watched her. Atalanta's eyes were fixed on the thicket

33

ahead. Her sun-bronzed hand reached over her right shoulder to take an arrow from the quiver, and the prince's heart beat faster. In all his life, he had never been so much aware of a woman.

She wasn't beautiful, not like the women he knew at home. Those women worked hard at beauty. Every fold of their long gowns, like every strand of their hair, was always perfect. They moved and looked like life-size dolls.

Atalanta didn't look like that. Her face, her arms, her legs were all much too thin. Her short tunic was wrinkled and dusty. Her long fair curls were tied back carelessly. The moment she moved, however, Meleager saw how graceful she was. "I'd love to see her dance," he thought.

Suddenly Atalanta looked up. She felt him watching her. She felt his admiration. "No," said her mind. "I serve Artemis. I have promised not to marry. I don't want a man watching me like that." Frowning, she moved to the right, further away from the crowd. Even though she did not look toward Meleager, she knew he was still looking at her, thinking about her. She could feel her face getting hot. She was not sorry she had made that promise to Artemis, not yet, but suddenly she knew that she might one day be very sorry indeed. Part of her wanted Meleager to notice every step she took.

As they stood together, the hunters formed a half-moon shape, fatter in the middle and trailing off to nothing at the end of each curve. "Forward," shouted Meleager, and the curved line of hunters began to push through the bush.

The boar could hear them coming. Suddenly it charged out of its hiding place. There was a fiery gleam in its bloodshot eyes, and its hide bristled with hairs that stuck straight out like spears. An elephant might have gloried in its gigantic tusks.

All the great heroes ran to meet the charge. At the front, one man tripped. "Aiee," he screamed. He had fallen on his own knife. Two men behind him could not get out of the way. They all tumbled on top of each other. The beast gored the nearest man with its great tusks and trampled the body. It chased another hero up a tree.

"Get back," yelled Atalanta. "Get away from it." Her bow was drawn, her arrow ready. At last she had a clear shot. She sank her arrow into the beast's head just behind one of its ears. It bellowed harshly, the hot foam flecking its broad shoulders. A man threw his javelin. The weapon missed its target, and the sharp point sank into a human chest. "Aah!" screamed the wounded man.

Again the animal charged. The nearest hunter swung his battle-axe. Too slow! He fell and was trampled under the pounding hooves.

Now Prince Meleager flung his javelin. He hit the boar's body on the right. The weapon pierced the tough hide and stuck there. The great beast whirled round and round, trying to get rid of the stick that was hurting so much. Meleager raced forward with his spear and plunged it deep under the boar's shoulder, all the way to its heart. It stood still for a moment, then crumpled and fell. At last the beast was dead.

"Hurrah!" they shouted. "Hurrah for Meleager!"

Meleager hardly heard the shouts. He was panting. Sweat trickled down his back. He looked over toward Atalanta. What a wonderful hunter she was!

Along with everybody else, Atalanta was looking at him. She was not shouting, but she nodded her head approvingly once, and then again.

Meleager felt that she was telling him, "Well done."

Some men laid out the bodies of the dead hunters. Meleager sent messengers to their families. "They died bravely," he said.

Quickly the hunters skinned the boar, talking as they worked.

"Huge, isn't it."

"Biggest I ever saw. No wonder it gave us such a fight."

"Some god must have sent it."

"That's for sure."

They gave the skin and tusks to Meleager, but Meleager took them right over to Atalanta. "You drew first blood, Atalanta," he said. "If we had left the boar alone, it would have died from the wound you gave it. You must have the tusks and skin."

Atalanta was delighted. Nobody but Telamon and Saurus had ever praised her skill before. "Thank you," she replied. "I'm sure Artemis guided my arm."

The other hunters were angry. "Wait a minute," they said. "That's not right."

Meleager's uncles were furious. "You killed the boar," they told him. "If you aren't going to keep the skin and tusks, you should give them to us."

"You didn't even wound it." Meleager was angry too.

"That doesn't matter. We're family. Giving the trophies to a woman — it's an insult to us." His uncle's fist clenched. He punched Meleager's jaw.

"Unh!" Meleager's fist hit out. He grunted as his uncle's chin jerked back.

"Look out," shouted Atalanta. Meleager looked around just in time to jump out of the way of his other uncle's knife.

Meleager's bloody spear lay on the ground in front of him. He grabbed it. As his uncle's knife flashed toward him for the second time, he lunged with the spear. It went through the older man's body. Now his other uncle fell on him. The two men traded punches. Meleager was younger, but he was very tired. His uncle got a wrestling hold on him and threw him to the ground. Strong hands went round Meleager's neck. It all happened so fast!

Everybody stared in horror, but nobody moved to try to stop the fight. Meleager could feel his eyeballs almost bursting. Soon he would be unconscious. Then he would be dead. "No," he told himself. "I won't let it happen." His arms came up wildly, his back bucked, and he was out from under. Now he threw his uncle to the ground and his own hands found their hold. Those hands did not let go.

At last Meleager stood up. He looked at his hands, and then at the bodies on the ground. His uncles had started the fight, but now both of them, his mother's brothers, were dead. Meleager gave a desperate groan. He threw himself on the ground and wept. That was the end of the great hunt.

"It's my fault," Atalanta told herself. "If I hadn't been here, it wouldn't have happened." She could not stop thinking about Meleager. One minute, he stood in front of her in triumph after killing the boar. The next, he lay weeping on the ground. His life was in ruins, and it had happened as quickly as that!

CHAPTER FOUR

A FATHER FINDS HIS DAUGHTER

For a long time Atalanta's father did not know that his daughter was alive. Iasus and his wife Clymene had no other children. Years went by, and they never talked about the baby girl who had been left on the hillside. When she was dying, Clymene said, "Husband, do this one thing: find out if our daughter lived or died. Sometimes a child is saved. We have both heard of such a thing."

"We never had a child," said Iasus angrily. But once reminded, he could not stop thinking. Nightmares invaded his sleep. He dreamed of wild dogs mauling a little body. "What's the matter?" he asked himself. "I didn't do anything wrong." But he could not stop the dreams. At last he called for his shepherd, the man who had taken away the baby, all those years ago.

"Go to the place where you left her," he

commanded. "Talk to anybody who lives nearby. See if you can hear anything about the child."

"Nobody lived anywhere close," replied the shepherd. "It was the loneliest place I could find. I'll go, of course, but don't expect me to find anything out. There won't be anything to find."

The shepherd was at the door when Iasus added, "Don't tell anybody I'm the one who's asking. I'm a rich man. Tell them it was your child. That way nobody's going to think they can get money out of me. Understand, I've got nothing to do with it."

"I understand," said the man. Poor baby, he thought, whether she lived or died I pity her.

"I've never travelled that way in all these years," he grumbled to his wife. "I didn't even want to think about it, not ever, and now I have to go up there and pretend I cast out my own child."

Luckily he did not have to pretend anything after all. On the second day, near evening, he came to a small house nestled in the hills. It was the only house he had seen for at least two hours. He had been climbing steadily all day, and he was tired. "I'm getting old," he grumbled. Just the same, he did not want to go up to the door. This was likely the closest house to the place where he had left the baby all those years ago. He did not want to think about it. He didn't want to ask questions.

He dragged his feet toward the door. At once the barking began, yips and yelps, along with a deeper sound: there were at least two dogs, and one of them was big. The door swung open. He didn't know it, but the goddess had directed his steps to Telamon and Merope.

"Take your evening meal with us," Telamon invited, settling the tired man by the warm hearth. "This is not a rich house, but we can give you food and a place to sleep in front of the fire. We don't often see a stranger." The door opened again as he spoke, and Atalanta stepped inside, carrying her bow. Slung over her shoulder along with her arrows were four large rabbits and a couple of partridges. The shepherd gulped. He closed his eyes and opened them again. The slim girl was still there, bending to put down the game she had killed.

"You wouldn't believe it," he told his wife later. "Looked just like the mistress when she was a girl. Darker – she lives out of doors – but I'd know her anywhere. Anybody would. She's got her father's hair, though; she didn't get those gold curls from her mum. Doesn't do a thing around the house, she spends her days hunting. She's got a wicked big bow and arrows! I don't know if I could bend her bow, let alone put an arrow to the string. She's the child the master is looking for, no doubt of that. I hope he's pleased."

The shepherd went to Iasus. "Your daughter is alive, and I have seen her," was his report. "She lives with hunters. She's a hunter herself, and a good one, they tell me. Strange life for a girl."

"She lives," concluded Iasus. "How fortunate that you returned today. I doubt Clymene will last the night. Now she can die in peace. The girl has turned out oddly, though, not the usual kind of daughter at all. I don't want anything to do with her."

As soon as he knew who and where his daughter was, however, Iasus kept thinking about her. Of course he had heard all about the great boar hunt and the honour that Atalanta had won. He sent for his shepherd again. "I've changed my mind. I'm proud of that girl," he said, "and I'm lonely. Atalanta must be almost old enough to be married, and I can afford it. Go to her. Tell her you come from her father. It's time she came home."

Atalanta was ready to hear him. She was still shocked by the way the hunt had ended. Meleager came often into her head. The pictures started with his loving look at her and his admiration of her skill, but moved horridly on to blood and ended quickly in despair. The ending stayed with her, his body pressed into the bloody earth, his fists like hammers, beating on the ground. She ran every day, but did not always carry her bow and arrows. A partridge could fly up right at her feet and she might feel no urge to shoot it. She did not rush right off to Iasus, all the same. The more she thought about his invitation, the more uncertain she became.

Atalanta tried saying the word, "Father," then "My father." She tried sentences. "My father sends for me. My father wants me. My father invites me to come home." At last she said, "My father cares about me."

She said it over and over again.

None of the words felt real. No picture rose in her mind to match what she said. She knew now that her father was a rich man named Iasus. He lived in a big house with many servants. What kind of man was he? He knew she was alive, he knew she was his daughter, and he wanted her. How strange it felt, after all those years.

Twice she put together food for her journey. Twice, she said goodbye, goodbye for now, to Telamon and Saurus and Merope. Twice she started down the path. The first time, the tears came as soon as she unlatched the gate. The second, she got a little further, but when she started to cry she couldn't stop. Her father's shepherd helped her back to the only home she knew. Now he was waiting again to guide her to Iasus.

One minute Atalanta wanted to leave immediately. The next, she wanted to stay with Telamon and Merope forever. "My father threw me out to die," she told herself. "He never looked for me in all those years. Why should I go to him now?"

"Telamon," she begged at last, "you have been like a father to me. What should I do?"

Telamon's big hand stroked Atalanta's tangled golden curls. "I'm going to miss you," he told her, "but you must go. It's the right thing to do." Atalanta, curled up beside his chair, cried quietly. This was her answer. Whatever happened afterwards, she had to meet her father, to stay with him for a while, to find out what he was like. She knew she had to find out.

CHAPTER FIVE

TROUBLE IN
THE FAMILY

Atalanta longed for her father to value her. She wanted him to be proud of her. She wanted him to watch her run and cheer for her. She wanted to tell him all about the boar hunt. Could she ever ask him why he didn't want her when she was born? Just thinking about it made the vomit rise in her throat. How could she be so angry? She wanted to whip him. She wanted to scream at him. She wanted to raise her bow and put an arrow through his neck.

"Give that knife to Medon here," Iasus had said, the first time they met. He gestured to the house servant. "A woman doesn't wear a knife."

Atalanta had handed over her little bronze knife with the silver handle. "Take very good care of it, Medon," she said. "It was a gift from my very best friend." She wanted to say, "It was a gift from my

who had made her first bow. They never told her what to do. She thought again about Iasus. She stopped running and looked toward the city where he lived. Her hands clenched themselves into fists.

"I'm a hunter, Father," she said. "You don't know me at all. I don't do household tasks." She talked as if Iasus were right in front of her. Her voice was loud and firm. "You don't care about me. Bad luck for you! You think I'll do anything you say? I won't. I don't need anybody to protect me. I've got Artemis."

At the back of Atalanta's mind was Merope's warning: "Artemis is a cruel goddess." But that warning was far back in her mind. It surfaced for a moment, and was pushed down again. She leaned forward to stretch her leg muscles before running on.

"I must keep my promise. I must not get married. I will be a runner. I will be a hunter." The words went round and round in Atalanta's head in tune with her thudding feet. She tried saying them out loud. They were not difficult to say. She could not make a picture of herself saying any of them to her father, all the same.

Suddenly rage boiled through her again. A huge old olive tree stood in her way. Instead of circling around it, she ran into it and started hitting it with both fists. A squirrel looked out of a hole in the tree. Atalanta's hand snaked out and grabbed the little animal. With a snap of her hands she broke its neck. "I hate you, Father, I hate you," she screamed. "You almost killed me once, and now you're trying to kill me again. I'll die cooped up indoors."

When at last she stopped beating the old tree, her hands were bruised and bleeding. She patted the rough bark. "Lucky you weren't really my father," she told it. Finally an idea came to her. Was it her own idea, or

had the goddess sent it? She went to talk to Iasus again.

"You'd like me to get married," she began. "I will agree to that, it's proper. But I need to respect the man I marry. If I'm going to respect him, he has to risk his life to win me."

"My goodness," said her father. "That's asking a great deal. What does he have to do?"

"Asking me to get married is asking a great deal from me too." Atalanta's response was sharp; then her voice softened. "Father, if I got married, I'd never be able to live the way I'm used to, the way of Artemis. I'm risking my life also." She paused. "I'll marry the man who can run faster than I can," she told Iasus. "I'll marry the man who can beat me in a race. It's not going to be safe or easy. When I win a race, I'll kill every man I've beaten. Anybody who wants to marry me has to want me so much he is ready to risk his life. Anybody who marries me has to be a better runner than I am."

Iasus clapped his hands. He had been afraid that Atalanta would refuse to get married, or would run away. What kind of father can't even marry off his own daughter? He would look like a fool. Everybody would laugh at him. Iasus liked his dignity. He was saved.

"You've had an inspiration, daughter. We'll be famous everywhere," he boasted. "I'll send messengers to proclaim the first race. You'll win me a worthy son-in-law. What else do I need to think about?" Iasus went on happily. "An important contest like this needs the right judge. Let me think who that should be. People have to trust him, don't they."

"Make sure his eyes are sharp," warned Atalanta. Thank the goddess I came late to this house, she thought, my father makes all the decisions here.

"I'll send for Melanion," Iasus announced. "He has settled many disputes. People know he will be fair."

I don't, thought Atalanta. I've never heard of him. Melanion. His name begins like Meleager. Melanion. Perhaps he'll be all right. I like the sound of his name.

Atalanta did not remind her father that she would have to lose the race before her father would win a son-in-law. "Artemis promised I would be the fastest runner in the world. Make sure that message is heard," she said. Now she felt safe. Nobody wants to die for a wife, she told herself.

She was wrong. Stories about Atalanta had spread throughout Greece. As the stories spread, they grew. Many men wanted to compete with the fastest runner in the world. Many men dreamed of triumph. She was young and lovely, so the stories said, and her father was rich. Furthermore, she was a woman favoured by a god: even to know her would be glorious. But it was the race that drew them. Some people are most deeply excited when they risk the highest stake of all, their life.

Men came from all over Greece to race against Atalanta. When they saw the black altar she had built, however, they hesitated. "Here is where I will sacrifice you after you lose the race," said Atalanta. She set her sharpening stone nearby and sharpened her long hunting knives. She sharpened the little bronze dagger. "The goddess Artemis will be pleased to drink your blood," she told them. Atalanta was trying to frighten the men. She did not want to kill them. She did not want to marry one of them either.

Her father entertained all the competitors royally. Atalanta noticed that most of them drank too much wine. She herself took only a sip. Most of them ate big helpings of roast meat. Atalanta ate very little. Some of the men were fat, some were thin, but not one of them had a wiry body like hers. "They have no discipline," she thought. "I don't think there's a runner here." Atalanta wasn't quite right. Many of the men were excited to see her, stirred by her presence. They drank too much out of nervousness. They wanted to talk to her, but at the look on her cold, set face, the voices died.

They talked to her father. Those who couldn't talk to her father talked to each other. Sometimes they stole little sideways glances at her.

Atalanta didn't know how they felt. Nobody even tried to talk to her. Her eyes stung. "I won't cry," she told herself angrily. "I don't need them – I don't need anybody." Prince Meleager had admired her. If the great hunt had ended differently, he might have loved her. Atalanta might have loved him, also. Artemis was a powerful protector, but there was nothing comfortable about her, nothing loving and warm. Atalanta shivered. She was cold right through to her bones.

The men talked together.

"Have you seen her run?"

"She runs with the hounds every morning. Nobody ever kept up with them the way she does."

"Do you think she'd really kill us?" they wondered. Atalanta looked as cold as snow.

"That altar looks ugly," one young man shuddered.

Another asked, "Have you felt her knives? I barely touched the edge of the little one, and look what it did to my finger." He held it up. The skin was cut right through.

"If I lose this race and have my throat cut on that black stone, who will remember me?" The speaker was thoughtful. "There is glory in winning, certainly, but I think that none of us can win. Atalanta serves Artemis," he said, "and Artemis is no friend to men."

But three men, Nikos, Maron, and Orthrus, decided to race with Atalanta. "Let's train together," they agreed. "We can run together and practise racing against each other." They ate carefully and went to bed early. All day they worked out and ran. After three weeks they were ready for the race.

Atalanta had not done any special training. She always ran for three or four hours in the morning. She did not eat rich food. She never drank much wine. "I'm ready to race any time," she told her father.

"You look ready," said Iasus. "I'll send for Melanion. He has agreed to be the judge." Iasus patted his own plump belly. "I wish my stomach was as flat as yours."

The day before the race, Atalanta sharpened her hunting knives one last time. "If you lose, you lose your lives," she warned the three men. "I'll slit your throats on the black altar of Artemis. Do you still want this race?"

Orthrus was scared. He wanted to drop out, but could not think of any reason that would not make him look like a coward. On the day of the race, however, his stomach did the thinking for him. He vomited again and again. "I can't race," he said. "I'm sick."

Everybody laughed at him. "Orthrus, we certainly believe you," his friends teased. "We know where this sickness comes from."

"Tease me if you like," said Orthrus. "Maybe I'll have grandchildren and you won't."

CHAPTER SIX

A DEADLY CONTEST

elanion arrived while the runners were getting ready. Iasus went to greet him. "It isn't easy, being judge of this race," he said. "Two men's lives are at stake today."

My fate, as well as theirs, is in Melanion's hands, thought Atalanta. She looked at him as closely as she could without being rude. He reminded her of Meleager, but an older Meleager, with much the same sturdy body. Meleager did not have dark hair, though, and Melanion's well-trimmed beard was black. His head was a mass of wiry curls, black except for two greying patches at his temples. His hands and muscular arms were heavy with black hair. On his wrist was a wide band of gold. His expression was alert and friendly. Smile wrinkles in his face showed that he smiled often, although he was not smiling now.

Melanion was watching Atalanta, just as she was watching him. They were intensely aware of each other. The silence was going on too long. "Where is the starting line?" asked Atalanta. She knew she needed to stop thinking about Melanion and Meleager and think only about the race.

"One moment, please." Melanion spoke politely. "The conditions of this race are very harsh. Will you really kill these two men if they lose? Is it such a crime to run slower than you?"

"It is no crime," said Atalanta. "They can easily withdraw. Artemis would be happy, and so would I, if I sacrificed two goats instead."

"I understand," replied Melanion. "Will you withdraw?" he asked Nikos and Maron.

The two young men stood proudly. They spoke almost at the same time: "Let's get on with the race."

The autumn sun would have been warm except for the cool breeze. The course was set through a meadow, around a little grove of oak trees, and back. The same line marked the beginning and the end.

Atalanta took the lead right away. Her feet hardly touched the earth. She kept a steady pace around the oak trees and back. She wasn't even out of breath when she crossed the finish line. "Atalanta, you are clearly the winner," declared the judge. Melanion's voice was husky. Atalanta's hand dropped to the little knife which she wore on her belt.

Everybody stared at the other two competitors. Nikos, puffing and gasping, staggered across the finish line. Maron sprawled on the ground not far from the grove of oaks. He dragged himself to his feet and ran for a few steps, only to trip and fall again. He could see Atalanta waiting. Now he did not even try to get up. Other men hauled him to his feet and half-carried him the rest of the way.

"I warned you," Atalanta told them. "This was your own choice. Now I call upon you to go as willing sacrifices to Artemis." Her heart ached. The little knife was cold and heavy in her hand.

"You don't want to kill them, do you," said Melanion sadly.

"No." Atalanta's voice was flat. "But I must. If I don't do exactly what I have promised, every man will race against me. There'll be no end to it. It's my life or theirs." She turned away. Her throat was tight. How can I bear to take these two young lives? she asked herself. "Help me, great Artemis," she begged.

Artemis appeared. She held her mighty silver bow. "I am Artemis of the gleaming arrows," she said, "and you are Atalanta, whose name means 'unswaying'." Her face was stern. "You made your choice, Atalanta, just as they made theirs. This is the result, and you cannot change it." Atalanta shuddered. Now she knew what Merope had meant, all those years ago. What had she said? "Sometime you may be sorry you did not learn to weave."

Under the eyes of Artemis, Atalanta forced herself to walk over to the black altar where Nikos and Maron waited. Priestesses of Artemis led them forward, then knelt with silver basins to catch their blood. "Think of them as deer, wounded deer," Atalanta told herself. "The only mercy I can offer is to be quick." The little knife flashed once, then again, and it was done. Atalanta watched the blood dripping from the darkened blade.

Melanion did not see the goddess. His eyes were fixed on Atalanta. She had tied up her hair for the race, but little tendrils of gold had escaped and clung damply around her pale cheeks. This woman had just killed two men, but she was not overcome by tears. She looked sadly at the blood, but showed no sign of faintness. Melanion could see a little pulse beating in her neck. He could feel the shudders that shook her body. He spoke without thinking. "This isn't right. It mustn't happen again. You must race against me, Atalanta. I shall win the race."

Atalanta had managed her gruesome task without weeping, but now tears streamed down her cheeks. "No," she said, "oh no, Melanion. I won't race against you."

CHAPTER SEVEN

MELANION
ASKS FOR HELP

Melanion was bewildered. When he wasn't near Atalanta, he thought he would withdraw from the race and go on a long journey. With luck, he would never see the woman again. At the same time, he was fascinated by her. His hands wanted to stroke her cheeks, to wind themselves into her golden curls. Her actions were harsh and cruel, yet her face had none of the hard and calculating lines that he would have expected. It was a child's face, open and trusting, except for the sudden flash of her fierce blue eyes.

"I don't know why I'm so set on this," Melanion told her. "Everybody says I'm a sensible man, and it's not sensible to race against you. I'm not sensible about you, Atalanta. I won't withdraw."

Atalanta had set the rules for the contest. Now she could not refuse to race

The grove was silent. With all his strength Melanion wished for the goddess to help him. Surely she would come. Surely the goddess of Love would help somebody who was so much in love. He heard nothing, though after some time his hair and tunic were touched by a little breeze, as if some great presence passed behind him, and the air grew deliciously warm. An image formed in his mind of three golden apples. At first he could see only the apples, shimmering and shining. Then he could see where they must be. He could smell them. He rose to his feet and walked around to the back of the goddess's statue. Again he knelt. He put his hand into a little rocky cleft. Slowly he drew out first one, then two more glorious apples, made surely of beaten gold.

The three apples were almost too heavy to hold. Melanion sat down and rested his full hands on his lap. Except for their weight and their rich colour, the apples looked real, dimpled at the stem and flower ends. Their scent was strong in his nostrils. Not one of them was a perfect ball; each was just a little elongated or off-centre, the way an apple might be when picked from a tree. Melanion laughed lightly as this thought came to him. Surely these apples never grew on any tree!

"Yes, they grew on a golden tree," a voice answered his thought, "my tree, with the gleaming leaves and the tinkling branches." It sounded all around him and within him at the same time: the golden voice of Love. Melanion could not see her, but he knew that the goddess was near.

"Take my golden apples," said Aphrodite. "They are my gift. Use them to win your bride."

"How?" cried Melanion. "Goddess, what must I do?"

"If you really love her, your love will tell you. Serve me faithfully, Melanion. Remember, I am Love."

"I will serve you always," cried Melanion.

The air was cold again. Melanion knew that the goddess was gone. She had given him what he needed, but he had to discover how to use her gift. He sat in front of her statue for a long time.

How odd! The apples had been so heavy when he sat down; now they were much lighter. Why? ... Now they were heavy again. How could that be? Heavy. Light. Heavy. Light. It was a long time before Melanion figured out that he was making the apples heavy or light by his thoughts. When he thought them heavy, they were heavy. When he thought them light, they were light. His plan leaped into his mind.

Melanion put the golden apples very carefully into his pouch. How light they are, he thought. His steps too were light as he returned.

"Telamon says we must race," said Atalanta. "I don't like it, but he thinks you have a chance. I hope he's right."

"Me too," said Melanion, but he didn't tell any of them about the golden apples. Magic talismans lose power when their secrets are betrayed.

Melanion and Atalanta walked back to Iasus's house more slowly than they had come. They were both feeling hopeful. They laughed and joked. "Will you hunt with me when we're married?" asked Melanion.

"Happily," Atalanta replied.

"Let's race tomorrow," said Melanion. "Have faith in me, dear Atalanta. I serve the goddess of Love. We will both run the best we can."

CHAPTER EIGHT

LOVE,
OR DEATH?

"I'll be the judge this time,"
said Iasus. "Melanion, my
friend, I hope you are more
sure of yourself than I am.
I'm worried about you."

"I'll do my best," said Melanion.
"Nobody can do more than that." He held
one golden apple in his right hand. The
other two were tucked into his belt.
They were firmly held, but would be
easy to remove when he needed them.

The course was the same as before.
The black altar still stood nearby, a grim
reminder. Everyone was very quiet. Iasus
gave the signal.

Light, thought Melanion, light. In his
mind he made an image of all three
apples. All the apples felt light. His
whole body felt light. He ran as Atalanta
had shown him, and marvelled. For a
short time, at least, he was keeping up
with her.

Atalanta could see that too. Without thinking, she lengthened her stride, just a little bit. Without thinking, she quickened her pace. Melanion saw her begin to pull ahead. Quickly he threw his apple. It rolled ahead of her and lay, glimmering and shimmering, just a little out of her path. Again without thinking, Atalanta altered direction slightly, stooped and picked it up.

Now Melanion had the task of keeping two lots of apples in his head, two pictures, as he ran. Atalanta's apple must be heavy; his own two apples must be light. He had practised the night before, but it was difficult, even when he was not running for his life. Atalanta was still ahead of him, but she was not gaining ground as fast as before.

Melanion got ready to throw his second apple as they approached the oak trees at the midway point. He threw it ahead just before he made his turn. If Atalanta was going to pick it up, she would have to run on further before she could start back. He didn't dare risk a glance at the apple to see what was happening. But when he had rounded the trees he could no longer see her ahead of him.

There is a spell on these apples, thought Atalanta. The first one weighed down her left hand. The second winked at her from the ground ahead. Could she leave it and go back after she won the race? No. When she won the race, she would have a sacrifice to perform. The thought skittered through her mind and vanished. Before she could go to look for the apple, somebody else would surely have picked it up.

The apple glittered. "Pick me up, pick me up," it seemed to call. She raced forward, stooped, caught it up and turned back to round the trees. But she had broken her pace and lost her concentration. The golden apples weighted down her hands. Melanion was well ahead.